U0086157

·大喜說故事系列·

Tashi
and the
DRAGON BREATH
大喜愚弄噴火龍

Anna Fienberg
Barbara Fienberg 著

Kim Gamble 繪

王秋瑩 譯

三民書局

Jack took Tashi outside to the **peppercorn** tree. They climbed up to Jack's special **branch** and when they were sitting comfortably, Jack said, 'Did you really meet a dragon?'

傑克帶大喜到外頭那棵黑胡椒樹下。他們倆爬上了傑克專用的樹枝，舒舒服服地坐好之後，傑克問，「你真的見過龍嗎？」

peppercorn [ˋpɛpɚˌkɔrn] 名 黑胡椒
branch [bræntʃ] 名 樹枝

'Yes,' said Tashi, 'it was like this. One day Grandmother asked me to go to the river to catch some fish for dinner.'

「是啊！」大喜說，「事情是這樣的。有一天，奶奶
要我到河裡捕些魚來當晚餐。」

'Was this in your old country?' asked Jack.

'Of course,' said Tashi. 'Grandmother doesn't **believe in** travel. Anyway, before I **set off**, Grandmother warned me, "Whatever you do, Tashi," she said, "don't go near the **steep**, **crumbly** bank at the bend of the river. The edge could **give way** and you could fall in. And," she added, "keep your eyes open for dragons."'

「這是在你老家時的事兒嗎？」傑克問。

「當然囉！」大喜說。「奶奶不喜歡旅行。總之，在我出發前，奶奶警告我說，『大喜啊，不管你做什麼事，可別靠近那河流彎曲的地方哪！那兒的堤岸又陡峭、又容易崩塌。那邊緣若是崩塌，你可能會摔下去哦。另外，』她又加了一句，『小心有龍啊！』」

believe in... 認為…是好的

set off 出發

steep [stip] 形 陡峭的

crumbly [`krʌmblɪ] 形 容易崩塌的

give way 崩塌，倒塌

'Dragons!' said Jack. 'What do you do if you meet a dragon?'

'Well, it was like this,' said Tashi. 'I walked across the **field** to the river and I caught five fish for dinner. I was just putting them into **a couple of buckets** of water to keep them fresh when I saw a cloud of smoke. It was **rising** from a **cave**, further up the mountain.'

「龍！」傑克說。「如果你遇到龍的話，你要怎麼辦？」

「這個嘛，事情是這樣的，」大喜說，「我穿過原野走到河邊，然後捉了五隻魚當晚餐。我把魚放進幾個裝了水的桶子裡來保持新鮮，就在這個時候，我看到一團煙從山洞中升起，飄向山頂。」

field [fɪld] 名 原野

a couple of 數個

bucket [ˋbʌkɪt] 名 水桶

rise [raɪz] 動 升起

cave [kev] 名 洞穴

'Ooah, did you run away home?' asked Jack.

'Not me,' said Tashi. 'I took my buckets and climbed up the mountain and there, sitting at the mouth of the cave, was the biggest dragon I'd ever seen.'

'Have you seen many?' asked Jack.

'I've seen a few **in my time**,' said Tashi. 'But not so close. And *this* dragon made me very **cross**.'

「哇！那你有趕緊跑回家嗎？」傑克問。

「我可不是這樣的人，」大喜說。「我提著水桶爬上山，在那裡，就在洞口，坐著一隻我所見過最巨大的龍。」

「你看過很多龍嗎？」傑克問。

「以前我有看過一些，」大喜說。「可是從沒這麼近看過。而且這隻龍讓我很生氣。

in one's time 在此之前

cross [krɔs] 形 不愉快的

He was **chomping** away at a **crispy**, dragon-breath-**roasted** pig.

"'That's my father's pig you're eating," I said.

"'I don't care," said the dragon. "I needed something to **cheer** me **up**."

牠正大口大口地吃著自己噴火烤的脆皮豬。

『「你吃的是我爸爸的豬耶！」』我說。

『「我才不管呢！」』那隻龍說。『「我需要找點樂子。」』

chomp [tʃamp] 勳 大口大口地咬 （=champ）

crispy [ˋkrɪspɪ] 形 酥脆的

roast [rost] 勳 烤

cheer...up 激勵（人）

'"You can't eat other people's pigs just because you **feel like** it," I told him.

'"Yes, I can. That's what dragons do."

『你不可以只因為你想要，就吃別人的豬啊！』我告訴牠。

　　『我就是可以。龍都是這麼做的。』

feel like　想要

'So I sat down next to him and said, "Why do you need cheering up?"

'"Because I'm **lonely**," said the dragon. "There was a time when I had a huge noisy family. We'd spend the days **swooping** over the countryside, **scaring** the villagers **out of their wits**, stealing pigs and **geese** and grandfathers, and roasting them with our dragon breath.

「於是我便坐到牠旁邊說，『那你為什麼需要找樂子呢？』」

「『因為我很寂寞，』龍說。『以前，我有個熱鬧的大家庭。白天的時候，我們突襲農村，把村民嚇得驚慌失措，然後偷走豬、鵝和老人，再噴火來烤他們。

lonely [`lonlɪ] 形 寂寞的

swoop [swup] 動 突襲

scare [skɛr] 動 驚嚇

out of one's wits 驚慌失措

goose [gus] 名 鵝（複數形geese）

Then we'd sing and **roar** all night till the sun
came up. Oh, those were the days!" The dragon
sighed then and I moved back a bit. "But Mom
and Dad grew old and died, and I **ate up** the rest
of the family. So now I'm the only dragon left."

然後我們整晚又唱又叫，直到太陽升起來。喔！多美好的時光啊！』龍嘆了一口氣，而我往後挪了一下下。『可是我爹娘老了死了，我又吃光了家裡其他的龍，所以現在只剩我一個了。』

roar [ror] 動 大聲吼叫

come up 上升

sigh [saɪ] 動 嘆息

eat up 吃光

'He looked straight at me and his **scaly** dragon eyes grew **slitty** and smoky. "A few **mouthfuls** of little boy might make me feel better," he said.'

'Oh no!' said Jack. 'What happened then?'
'Well, it was like this. I quickly stood up, ready to run, and the water in my buckets **slopped** out over the side.

「牠直直地盯著我看，牠那對長鱗的龍眼漸漸瞇了起來，而且還冒起了煙。『吃幾口小男孩的肉應該會讓我覺得好一點。』牠說。」

「噢！不！」傑克說。「然後發生了什麼事呢？」

「這個嘛，事情是這樣的。我趕緊站了起來，準備逃跑，水桶裡的水就濺了出來。

scaly [`skelɪ] 形 有鱗的
slitty [`slɪtɪ] 形 狹長的
mouthful [`mauθ,ful] 名 一口
slop [slɑp] 動 溢出

"**"Look out!**" cried the dragon. "**Watch your step**! Dragons don't like water, you know. We have to be careful of our fire.""

「『小心啊！』龍大叫了起來。『小心走好！你知道龍是不喜歡水的！我們得小心我們的火。』」

look out 小心
watch one's step 小心行進

'Aha!' said Jack.

'Yes,' said Tashi. 'That gave me an idea. So I **looked** him **in the eye** and said, "You're not the last dragon, oh no you're not! I saw one only this morning down by the river. Come, I'll show you, it's just by the bend."

「啊哈！」傑克說。

「沒錯！」大喜說。「這讓我靈機一動呢！於是我看著牠的眼睛說，『你才不是最後一隻龍呢！你才不是呢！就在今天早上我才在下面的河邊看到一隻龍。來，我指給你看，就在河彎那裡。』

look...in the eye 直視…的眼睛

'Well, the dragon grew all hot with excitement and he followed me down the mountain to the bend in the river. And there it was all steep and crumbly.

'"He can't be here," said the dragon, **looking around**. "Dragons don't go into rivers."
'"This one does," I said. "Just **look over** the edge and you'll see him."

「唔，那隻龍興奮、激動了起來，跟著我下山往河灣走去。那裡又陡峭又容易坍塌。

『牠不可能在這裡的，』龍四下看了看，『龍是不會下水的。』

『這隻龍會，』我說。『只要去岸邊瞧瞧，你就會看到牠了。』

look around　四處看看

look over　環視

'The dragon **leaned** over and **peered** down into
the water. And he saw another dragon!
He breathed a great **flaming** breath. And the
other dragon breathed a great flaming breath.

He **waved** his huge scaly wing. And the other dragon waved his huge scaly wing.

「龍探出身去往水裡一看。牠看到了另外一隻龍！

牠噴出了一道灼熱的火燄；那隻龍也噴出一道灼熱的火燄。

lean [lin] 動 彎曲上身

peer [pɪr] 動 凝視

flaming [`flemɪŋ] 形 冒火燃燒的

牠揮動牠長著鱗片的大翅膀；而那隻龍也揮了揮牠長著鱗片的大翅膀。

wave [wev] 動 揮動

'And then the steep crumbly bank gave way and *whoosh!* the dragon **slid** *splash!* into the river.

「接著，那陡峭又容易崩塌的堤岸咻地一聲塌陷了！那隻龍噗通一聲滑進了河裡。

whoosh [(h)wuʃ] 感 呼的一聲

slide [slaɪd] 動 滑倒（過去式 slid [slɪd]）

splash [splæʃ] 副 噗通一聲

'An **enormous** dragon-shaped cloud of **steam** rose up from the river, and the water **sizzled** as the dragon's fire was **swallowed** up.'

「一股巨大的龍形蒸氣從河裡升起，龍的火燄被水淹沒時，河水還發出了嗞嗞聲。」

enormous [ɪ`nɔrməs] 形 巨大的
steam [stim] 名 蒸氣
sizzle [`sɪzḷ] 動 發出嗞嗞聲
swallow [`swɑlo] 動 淹沒

'**Hurray**!' cried Jack. 'And *then* did you run away home?'

'Yes,' said Tashi. 'I certainly did run home because I was late. And sure enough Grandmother said, "Well, you **took your time** catching those fish today, Tashi."'

「好吧！」傑克大叫。「那你後來有趕快跑回家嗎？」

「有啊！」大喜說。「我的確是用跑的回家，因為我太晚回家了。晚到奶奶一定會說，『啊喲，大喜，你今天可是慢條斯理地捉魚喲！』」

hurray [həˋre] 感 好吧
take one's time 慢慢來

'So that's the end of the story,' said Jack sadly.
'And now all the village was safe and no-one
had to worry any more.'

「故事就這樣結束了，」傑克遺憾地說。「現在全村都安全了，大家都不用再擔心了。」

'Well, it wasn't quite like that,' said Tashi. 'You see, the dragon had just one friend. It was Chintu the **giant**, and he was as big as two houses **put together**.'

'*Oho!*' said Jack. 'And Chintu is for tomorrow, right?'

「嗯，還不光是這樣呢！」大喜說。

「是這樣的，那隻龍正好有一個朋友，就是巨人青頭，他足足有兩棟房子疊起來那麼高大。」

「喔！」傑克說。「那你明天要說青頭囉，對不對？」

giant [`dʒaɪənt] 名 巨人

put together 把…加起來

'Right!' said Tashi.

「沒錯！」大喜說。

And the two boys **slipped** down from the tree
and **wandered** back into the house.

然後，這兩個男孩從樹上滑了下來，慢慢地走回家。

slip [slɪp] 動 滑
wander [ˋwɑndɚ] 動 閒逛

專為青少年朋友設計的百科全書

人類文明小百科

行政院新聞局推介
中小學生優良課外讀物

人類文明小百科，全套共十七冊

為臺灣的新生代開啟一扇知識的窗

歐洲的城堡

法老時代的埃及

羅馬人

希臘人

希伯來人

高盧人

樂　器

史前人類

火山與地震

探索與發現

從行星到眾星系

電　影

科學簡史

奧林匹克運動會

音樂史

身體與健康

神　話

小普羅藝術叢書

·小畫家的天空系列·

活用不同的創作工具

靈活表現各種題材

讓青少年朋友動手又動腦

創造一個夢想的世界

國家圖書館出版品預行編目資料

大喜愚弄噴火龍 / Anna Fienberg,Barbara Fienberg
著;Kim Gamble繪;王秋瑩譯.－－初版一刷.－－臺
北市；三民，民90
　　面;公分--(探索英文叢書.大喜說故事系列;2)
中英對照
ISBN 957-14-3412-4　(平裝)
　1.英國語言－讀本

805.18　　　　　　　　　　　　90002836

網路書店位址　http://www.sanmin.com.tw

© 　大喜愚弄噴火龍

著作人　Anna Fienberg　Barbara Fienberg
繪　圖　Kim Gamble
譯　者　王秋瑩
發行人　劉振強
著作財　三民書局股份有限公司
產權人　臺北市復興北路三八六號
發行所　三民書局股份有限公司
　　　　地址／臺北市復興北路三八六號
　　　　電話／二五○○六六○○
　　　　郵撥／○○○九九九八－－五號
印刷所　三民書局股份有限公司
門市部　復北店／臺北市復興北路三八六號
　　　　重南店／臺北市重慶南路一段六十一號
初版一刷　中華民國九十年四月
編　號　S 85580
定　價　新臺幣壹佰柒拾元
行政院新聞局登記證局版臺業字第○二○○號

ISBN　957-14-3412-4　(平裝)